The Marquis and the Mistress

House of Lords Book 2

1Night Stand series

By
Dominique Eastwick

Copyright © 2016 by Dominique Eastwick
ISBN: 978-1-61333-981-7
Cover art by Cora Graphics

Published by Decadent Publishing Company, LLC
Look for us online at:
www.decadentpublishing.com

Praise for *The Marquis & the Mistress*

All I can say is wow! My expectations were blown away. It was like a novel all wrapped up and packaged with a great big bow... Yes, I am totally vested in this couple. So much so, I'm up at 1 am writing how much I adored this story. ~ Amazon Reviewer

This short Regency is perfect for an evening's getaway from the mundane! ~ Amazon Reviewer

The chemistry brings the characters together, but it is the love that will keep them together. I hope there will be more in the series! ~ Amazon Reivewer

I loved this story and how Ms. Eastwick has given new life to the era. ~ Amazon Reviewer

~A Note from the Author~

Dear Reader,

I never thought there would be a second book after
The Duke and the Virgin. Certainly didn't think I
would create a series out of it. But here it is. So I
bring Madame Eve back to Regency England to mend
the broken heart of a Lord who wants nothing more
than for his mistress to be his wife, it is unfortunate
she doesn't feel the same…or does she?

Happy Reading!

Dom

Dedication

Dedicated to all the readers who take the jury with me in every book I write and every book they read.

Special thanks to Val and Kate for pulling the very best from me and to Dawn, Tam, Emmeline, Dwayne, and Patty for always loving me.

As always thank you to Nadine who always pushes me to stop procrastinating.

Chapter One

"I'm out." Lord Simon James Winston, 7th Marquis of Breckinridge threw his cards down and shoved his chair from the table. He could not beat Foxhaven. The damned duke was on one of his winning streaks.

Simon and Wolfe Thane, Duke of Foxhaven, had known each other since before they'd been in long pants, yet some things never changed. When boredom struck Wolfe, he never lost. Whether at cards like this evening, a foolish dare in college, or fisticuffs, which could happen if Lord Railey didn't shut his trap soon, nothing bad befell his grace.

Unfortunately, the other men of their party weren't quite as smart picking up the clues. The indications were laid before them like a map. First, Wolfe's lack of interest in the near brawls at Parliament earlier in the week, which he'd walked out of when asked to interfere. Followed by being nowhere to be seen at his mother's annual ball. Simon finally found him in the

1

library, alone, reading a book about planting in the Colonies. But the true sign lay at the gym; no one would go against him. After men left the ring black and blue, at least they'd gotten that message.

Although the men didn't appear to understand his *I could not care if I win or lose* attitude this night, a sure sign they were about to lose every shilling they had on them.

Lord Andrew Masterson, Earl of Windenshire, studied his cards before turning his attention to Simon as if debating what to do. Surely, he had something in his hand to keep him in another round. But if the earl wanted to throw in some blunt, who was Simon to care? Of all the men in their group, the earl had held his title the longest. In fact, at a mere week of age, he'd become the ninth earl of Windenshire, as his father died shortly after Andrew's birth. As the eighth earl had been close to ninety, it had shocked everyone that he had made it as long as he had, and that he'd procured an heir to boot. But, according to rumor, Andrew was the spitting image of the previous earl in his younger years, leaving no one to question paternity. "I'm out, too, damn it."

That left Viscount Jonathon Railey, whose father ruled his lands, servants, and his family with an iron fist. It was rumored, half in jest, he would never die because he was unwilling to give up any of his power to anyone. All the while, he'd been so concerned his title would pass to his brother's family, he kept breeding until he had his heir and nine spares. The man was nothing if not thorough in making sure his line would carry on. For most men, two sons would have been enough. But not for the Earl of Stockton, who had harped on everything from the Black Plague's return, to the possibility of another war with the Colonies, this time with an invasion of England. Between war and disease, his boys were sure to all die gruesome deaths. Unfortunately, ensuring such security in the line led to a shortage of money to spread to all the siblings. Jon had money, but the younger the son, the smaller the allowance. Simon suspected Jonathan had been taking care of his younger siblings while the older ones tried hard to make a living the only way the aristocracy could. So, he had more reason than most to throw in his cards unless he held the perfect hand. But like always, the man goaded Wolfe into playing higher and higher. This had been the pair's *modus operandi* since their days in Eton.

"Oh, the puppy is playing hard tonight." Wagging his eyebrows, Jonathan picked up his cigar and puffed.

"Jon, keep your head," Simon warned.

Wolfe hated being called a pup. Even the future duke wasn't immune to the bullying handed out to most youngsters on campus. Give someone a name like Wolfe and it added fodder to the fire for jealous second and third sons who had no certain future.

Wolfe grinned, showing his white teeth. "Don't warn him now. This is the most fun I have had all night. Hell, all week."

Ah, bollocks. Simon downed the remaining brandy, alerting the servant who appeared ready to fall asleep on his feet that his glass was empty. "Refill all the glasses, William, and then take yourself to bed. We can manage without you for the night."

"Thank you, sir."

The hands kept going, the bids higher and higher. Andrew rose long enough to bring the brandy to the table. When Wolfe pushed all his coins into the center of the table, Simon choked on his drink. Jonathon waited a second before pulling out a letter still closed with a rich royal red seal. Unfortunately, between the angle and lighting, Simon couldn't make out the insignia.

"What, pray tell, is that?" Wolfe demanded.

"An exclusive evening with a woman chosen specifically for you by Madame Eve."

"Who?" Wolfe asked in typical bored, droll manner.

But Simon heard something like pique in his voice. He doubted it had to do with the item as much as the reason Jonathon might have purchased it.

"Madame Eve. She arranges the perfect mates for people for an evening. I can't believe you've never heard of her, Your Grace," Andrew said, adding fuel to the growing fire already annoying Wolfe.

He glared at Andrew. "I have never needed to hire

someone to get laid, unlike others in this room."

"Yes, well some of us weren't blessed being a duke, either," Jonathon muttered.

"Throw your date in the kitty then, and show your hand."

Jonathan smiled, tossing down four of a kind. Reaching in to take the winning pile, he paused when Wolfe placed each card in his own hand, one by one, face up on the table. "A royal flush."

Andrew roared with laughter. "And that is why, when Simon throws his cards in, so do I."

"It appears your perfect date is going to spend the night of her dreams with me—you know—the duke." But Wolfe didn't reach out to grab the pot, in fact, stayed put, staring at the envelope as if it might bite him.

Simon sat at the round table long after the last cigar was snuffed out and the last of his friends stepped into their carriages. The four of them had been meeting for a weekly card game for the last seven seasons, providing they were all in town. Over the last two seasons, it had been his habit to leave immediately after his friends. No matter what the hour of his arrival at the townhouse he'd bought for their liaison, his lover waited for him. He ached for a woman's touch, but not any woman would do.

He tapped the cigar cutter on the table. Closing his eyes, he tried to focus on anything but the soft curves of the widow Chandra Mallory, his former lover of the last two years. She'd finished things weeks ago and refused to speak with him. He only knew she hadn't been at any social event in weeks and when he had his driver ride by her place, the knocker was no longer on the door, a proper indication she wasn't at home. Which left him unsure where she would go, as the lands of her late husband had been entailed to his nephew, Marcus Mallory, who had promptly thrown Chandra out on her bottom.

But the Mallory London townhome she and her late husband had lived in hadn't been entailed. That and a small allowance kept her, if not in extravagance, at least in comfort. It took every amount of willpower not to shove his fist down the nephew's throat each time Simon saw him in Parliament. The half-wit had somehow managed to get elected to his uncle's seat in the House of Commons. Forcing the simpleton into Simon's proximity.

Hearing Mallory talk about the swiftness with which he'd cleaned his house once it had been determined the widow wasn't carrying an heir had taxed Simon's already-thin patience. But unless he wanted to raise eyebrows and cause tongues to wag, Simon had to play it close to the cuff. Yet every time a conversation had ended with her wistful, sad voice about the house that had been her home for a decade, he'd wanted to land his knuckles, with great force, on the jerk's nose. Chandra had once told Simon about the humiliation of having to prove she wasn't with child, and when the heir had announced she was no longer welcome in his home, he'd given her that day to get out.

Simply thinking about her made Simon hard, forcing him to adjust in his seat. *This has to end.* But no other woman seemed to do, though he'd danced with other women at various balls since, walked with them in the gardens at those balls, hell, even kissed a few. Not one of them brought his cock to attention.

Perhaps contacting Madame Evangeline might prove just the thing. If she found a woman to arouse him for even one night, he could move on with his life. And as long as no one but he, his date, and the elusive Madame Eve knew about it, no one would be the wiser. Time to try something new. Anything to get the images of Chandra out of his dreams and purge her from his heart would be a welcome addition. Decision made, he threw the cigar cutter onto the table.

***

Chandra walked around the table one more time. The beautifully laid dining table had been set with the finest bone china. Elegant silver and crystal sparkled in the candlelight and held every delicacy she loved, from oranges to chocolate sweets. Her stomach rumbled, reminding her she should have eaten the food Cook had put in front of her that afternoon. Instead, she'd sat at her desk, debating sending the letter she had written to Madame Eve, declaring she could not make her date that evening.

But in the end, her had decision changed again. While strolling through the park, she had caught a glimpse of her ex-lover, Lord Breckinridge. As always, he'd dressed in the highest fashion: well-tailored clothing that even from across the park showed his muscular physique. Memories of him making love to her had forced her to sit on the nearest bench for fear her legs would go out beneath her. From the safety of seat, she had watched him. It was doubtful he had seen her, but if he had, he'd done an admirable imitation ignoring her. Yet, he had stopped and chatted with every marriage-mart mama and their slew of young daughters. The eligible marquis would make a fine husband to any young miss.

Chandra knew only too well how fine a catch he was. Well-read, well-versed in the arts and in bed, he made a woman believe herself a Greek goddess. He'd worshipped Chandra's body and played to her deepest emotions and darkest fantasies. She placed a supporting hand against her corseted belly as if she could hold back the emotions thinking of him caused. Simon was in the market for a wife; the time had come for him to create an heir; and as surely as Chandra knew that, she also knew she would never be his marchioness.

No matter how much she wanted to be.

Chandra had sold some jewels Simon had given her as a parting gift, the memory of receiving them too painful. So, it only seemed fair to use the proceeds of that sale to allow herself one night of pleasure to forget him. When an unmarked coach had pulled in front of her home at precisely eight that evening, she had entered, head held high, and ridden to a townhouse procured by Madame Evangeline for her date. But no one else knew where Chandra had gone tonight. None of her inner circle, at any rate. Not her staff, her friends, and most certainly not her sister, who had married a pastor.

Now, in this room, she fought to keep the jitters at bay. Her common sense fought an uphill battle with the urge to run and with all her bravado, she longed to be anywhere else but here. She could do this. No, this *had* to happen. She would have a single night with a stranger and when morning came, she could walk away and move on. She had convinced herself of that. But now, in the large quiet building on the outskirts of London, she wasn't so sure.

A soft knock preceded the maid entering with another plate of food. "Ma'am, your date has arrived. If you should need anything further, pull this cord, and I will come up." She set aside the ornate curtain to display a hunter-green cord. "The bell will ring only in my room. For any reason, call for me."

"Can I ask you a question?" Chandra's hands shook, as did her voice. She clasped them before her in an effort to control her nerves.

The maid paused in her duties. "Yes, ma'am."

"Have you worked here long?"

"Yes, ma'am, going on two years now."

Chandra bit her lip. "Have there been a lot of these—dates?"

"Not a lot, ma'am, but they are steady in coming

to us. Let me assure you no woman has yet touched that cord." The maid smiled. "Unless you ring, I will see you in the morning to help you dress."

"Thank you...?"

"Milly."

"Thank you, Milly."

The maid turned at the sound of footsteps on the stairs at the same time Chandra did. "I will go out the bedchamber door once he is inside. No person here will see you both, for your safety and reputation."

Chandra nodded. Two distinct male voices chatted on the other side of the door, hushed, so she couldn't discern what was said. She turned away, keeping her mystery gentleman behind her until she could garner the courage to face her night.

The door creaked open and closed on a soft click. She couldn't hear anything over the beating of her heart. Hoping for strength to stay on her feet, she gripped the top of the chair closest to her with gloved fingers until the blood ceased to flow through them. With her other hand, she pressed her stomach to calm the butterflies churning within. Taking a steadying breath, she closed her eyes and pivoted toward the newcomer.

"What the hell are you doing here?" The angry voice was full of male self-righteousness.

Looking up at the gentlemen, Chandra hid her shock, but only just. Anger she could deal with. It gave her time to get the situation under control. "I imagine, Simon, darling, for the same thing you are."

"Madame Eve was wrong. Perfect date, my ass," he muttered.

He paced the small dining room like a caged animal, cursing the air blue. He paused to remove his waistcoat, throwing it on a Queen Anne chair in the corner, only to pick it up again and slam it down, over and over. Once the poor coat had taken quite a beating, Simon returned to his pacing.

"Are you quite finished or do you plan to beat your waistcoat next?"

He glared at her. "Be happy I am venting my spleen on fabric and not shaking you to within an inch of your life."

She raised an eyebrow. "Pardon me?"

"Do you have any idea how reckless this adventure of yours is? You had no idea where you were going and I would bet you didn't tell a single soul, so no one is expecting you any time soon. Not to mention it could have been any rake, rogue, or scoundrel waiting for you."

"Instead it was only one rake, rogue, and scoundrel."

"Scoundrel! I never once treated you with anything but respect."

His fury dared her to argue. She could have brought up the insulting gift of gaudy jewelry he'd sent her, but then she would have to explain what she'd done with it and stopped herself, if only because she feared the furniture might feel his wrath next.

"God, I should return you home now," he said.

"We ended things weeks ago. I am not your responsibility." As soon as she spoke the words, she knew they had been the wrong ones. Simon appeared to have had the wind taken out of his sails. "Simon, I didn't—"

Raising a palm, he stopped her. "Chandra, I am fine. Simply lost my head for a bit." Striding to the table, he grabbed the wine and poured a glass. Under normal circumstances, he would have offered her one first. Instead, he gulped down two before grabbing the bottle on its own and stomping over the chair in the corner, evidently content to drink directly from the source. "Why don't you call your servant liaison and tell her to call your carriage around to take you home?"

Her brain advised her to do what he suggested before things moved out of her control. But her heart didn't much care what was sensible. "I will, but they went to a lot of trouble to make this night special. It would be rude not to eat the dinner laid out for us, at least."

Simon sat with his elbows on his knees, staring at the wine bottle in his grasp. For long minutes, he didn't answer or acknowledge her. When his gaze finally met hers, she couldn't read his thoughts. In the past, his emotions and thoughts had been like an open book to her. Now, he only gave her a blank stare and shrugged.

He stood to his full, imposing six-foot height then, every long stride toward the end of the elegant dining table emphasizing legs in tight-fitting pants. Images flooded her of the first time he had walked across a crowded ballroom in order to sign her dance card. Being only recently out of mourning for her husband, she had not planned to dance. Rather than being waylaid by her announcement, however, Simon had stayed.

As they'd strolled around the ballroom she'd found herself relaxing, and by their third turn, something about him convinced her to take a walk in the gardens when he offered.

Perhaps it had been the champagne, or maybe the romantic lighting easing her inhibitions as they moved farther into the private grounds of the estate. Or, perhaps, after a year of mourning, she longed to have a man touch her again. But there, in his embrace under the moonlight, her blood seemed to boil and she'd cursed her clothing as it proved a barrier against what she wanted most: his touch. Erotic images of his hands on her breast, his mouth against her pale skin, had left her shaken before he did more than brush his lips across hers. Once he'd kissed her, she'd nearly let him take her, uncaring if anyone came across them. All she had been able to focus on were his strong hands and the way his kisses weakened her knees.

She'd loved her husband. He'd been a sweet, considerate man. Yet, ten minutes spent in the arms of the notorious rogue, Simon, and she'd realized she had never felt passion before. Lord Breckinridge could very well be dangerous to her wellbeing.

"Chandra." His voice cut through the fog of memories. "Are you all right?"

Nodding, she stood across the small table from him and gestured at the food. "What would you like, my lord?"

"You don't have to serve me."

"It's all right. I want to."

He shrugged and took a seat, placing the white napkin in his lap. She reached for his plate, careful not to make contact with his hands, and picked the foods he loved by memory. When she handed it to him, his fingers brushed hers and she bit back a gasp as a shock of electricity sparked through her.

His eyes met hers, the familiar desire within them taking her breath away. She expected him to put his meal to the side and pull her into his arms. But he wouldn't do anything like that. Not ever again.

They ate in relative quiet, the only sound the occasional scraping of silverware on china. The food might have been the best, but she tasted nothing.

"Simon, I'm sorry."

"What exactly are you sorry for?" He placed his fork on the table. The man before her bore no emotional resemblance to the angry ex-lover who had walked into the room earlier. This gentleman was the marquis she knew, always in control, and how he had been during the first month of their relationship. Though he gave all of himself in bed, he closed off completely when out of it. Only into the second month had she learned anything about his family.

She met his gaze. "I'm sorry if I hurt you."

"In what way? Because you paid to have sex with a stranger rather than having sex with me, as my wife?"

There it was, out in the open. Her rejection of his marriage proposal. In his mind, she had taken his heart and stomped it into the ground. Yet nothing could be further from the truth—she cherished everything about him. Her love for him had caused her to turn down the one thing she wanted more than anything else, the one thing she could never be. His wife.

Chapter Two

She stared at him across the table, as if what he'd blurted didn't prove what an idiot he was. He should have followed his gut and cried off from the evening. Yet a letter had arrived early in the afternoon, right as he'd been about to send a message to Madame Eve about his decision to cancel. Her letter had spoken to all the reasons the evening could prove to be fruitful. No way could the secretive Madame Eve have known about his two-year relationship with Chandra. No one knew. His friends believed he'd had a long-standing mistress, but never once had he hinted who his bedmate might be.

When he had first caught sight of Chandra in that ballroom, his body had reacted instantly, every fiber of his being screaming to claim her and make her his. Taking her into the gardens had been an action of insanity. Privacy be damned, he'd been close to pulling up her skirts and taking her right there. Passion had never come so fast or so powerful to him.

After they had spent their first evening together, he'd been unable to walk straight the next day. She'd ridden him like a prize stallion at Newmarket. Her appetite met his, stroke for stroke. The more he gave, the more she took. The passion in the well-bred woman had surprised him and by morning, he'd known it would take many more nights to assuage the burning desire she fueled.

As the days became months, there'd been no way he would ever get her out of his system. She was an addiction he had no intention of giving up. He'd bought a place near hers, on a side street where few of the haute ton would ride by. Servants came only when the house was unoccupied, allowing he and Chandra the freedom of privacy. Over the last few months, he had spent more time at the townhouse than at his family abode on Grosvenor Square.

Chandra had worked with him, through the bills he'd had before the House of Lords, as well as helped deal with some issues on his lands in the north. She had a way of taking his speeches and letters and making them personable, less stern, and at the same time relaying their serious nature. He and Chandra complemented each other, she soft and giving, he stern, yet fair. He in turn assisted with her finances, allowing her to get the most from what was left to her. Yet she refused to take money from him. She would give every shilling she had to others, so he'd set up safeguards in order for her to be charitable without it beggaring her. But most of the time they spent in each other's arms, reading, talking, or simply sitting in companionable silence.

"Simon?"

"What?" Shaking his head to clear the memories, he walked to the closed door at the other end of the room. He opened it and cursed upon seeing the large four-poster bed, draped in rich red-velvet bedding. Images of her stripped bare, her pale skin in contrast to the deep colors, hardened his cock. "It appears Madame Eve thinks of everything."

"There is also a bathing chamber attached to that room."

"Imagery I didn't need." Because if thinking of her naked in bed wasn't enough, her in a warm bath certainly was.

She touched his shoulder. The simple gesture broke the small thread holding his self-control. Quicker than she could blink, he twisted and pulled her roughly into his arms. Claiming her mouth, he darted his tongue inside when she opened on a surprised gasp. He wound a hand around her waist and jerked her close so she felt how much he wanted her, while threading fingers into her hair, yanking at the pins holding it in its perfectly-coifed bun.

He waited for her to shove him away. Slap his face. Anything to give him a hint he had stepped over the line. But, with a deep moan, she circled her arms around his neck, drawing her small frame up for even closer contact. He deepened the kiss, backing her into the wall, tugging at the layers of fabric in her skirt and gathering them up past her hips. He placed his knee between her bare legs. The damned woman wore no undergarments.

The idea both angered and aroused him.

Forcing the thought she had come prepared to sleep with another man to the back of his mind, he focused on the fact she was in his arms again. She arched against his linen pants, her arousal burning through the thin cloth, driving his hunger for her to heights he had never believed possible, the blood in his veins nearly boiling. Her awkward fingers worked the buttons of his breeches until she had freed his cock. The erection demanded attention and he was unable to think with the rush of blood to his nether regions.

He tore his mouth from hers. "Tell me to stop."

She shook her head and, with hands that didn't seem to touch enough to satisfy him, she urged his insatiable desires further, telling him she was as lust-filled as he.

Gripping her bottom, he raised her up until his cock sat at the entrance of her wet pussy. She whimpered but didn't stop him. Still, he waited, needing her permission. He could never live with himself if she regretted this in the morning.

"Tell me what you want."

Again, she shook her head.

"Say it," he commanded in the way that made

lesser lords run for cover.

"Take me now, please?" she said into his shoulder. "Simon, I need you."

"Shall we both burn in hell," he said and lowered her, positioning his cock so he could slip inside her. With a groan, he took her mouth and surged upward until she could take no more of him. Using the wall for support, he retreated before surging in again. He built the rhythm and she matched his strokes, keeping time with his beat. Wrapping her legs around his hips, she dug her heels into the small of his back.

"Simon, please." Her breath, hot and soft, sent shudders down his spine. "Not here, not like this."

Nodding, he toed off his shoes, thankful he'd decided not to wear his Hessian boots for the evening. He kicked his pants to the side before drawing away from the wall. Step by slow, excruciating step, he moved them toward the bed, every stride forcing her down on his cock. Ten paces had never seemed so long. After setting her ass on the edge of the high bed, he eased away enough to unfasten his waistcoat, yanked the neckcloth off, tossed it aside, then lifted the shirt over his head.

With every item of clothing out of the way, he focused on how to get her out of hers. He decided to start with the petticoat, the fragile fabric tearing easily and landing in a heap on the floor. She showed no signs of caring. He worked the lacings of her dress until they finally gave way and he cursed, wishing to tear the rest of her garments off as well until she was glorious and naked with him.

He eased the dress over her shoulders, trapping her arms to her sides while he worked the corset from her body. Once free of her stays, she lay back, spread out before him, naked to the waist and unable to move her arms.

"Simon, please, release my arms."

"Not yet." He took one of her pert nipples into his mouth and sucked. Wordlessly, she squirmed and arched, telling him what she wanted with each motion. Aiming to please her, he worked one breast and then the other until she shook with uncontrolled need.

"Let me touch you," she begged.

"No."

"But—"

"I am going to brand myself on you tonight. Do you understand?"

She nodded.

He gently bit the underside of her breast. "Say it."

"Yes, I understand."

Working up her body to her lips, he kissed her with so much passion, words weren't needed to tell her what how he missed her. She had to know, had to understand. In the morning, they would either leave betrothed or he would walk away without a backward glance. After offering for her once, it went against convention for him to do so again. But, convention be damned, he loved the woman, and if asking once more gained him what he needed, he would do it. To hell with society and its fucking rules.

Throwing her head back, she both cursed and praised his name. She shifted her shoulders, desperate to free her arms. But he could remain in charge only if her long, able fingers stayed off his body. He eased away from her long enough to flip her on her stomach. Ignoring another plea to free her arms, he gathered her skirts up her silk-stockinged thighs. His free hand ran up the outside, excruciatingly slowly, relearning what his memories hadn't given justice to. Finally, she lay bare to him.

His touch never left her ass. "Do you remember the first time I spanked you, Chandra, how you cried for more? How beautifully red your ass was, so hot to touch. You were so wet. No matter how many times I took you that night, it was never enough."

Eyes shut tight, she nodded and bit her lip as his palm, came in contact with her buttock. The sound, crisp and sharp, vibrated through the room. "Yes, I remember."

"Do you want me to spank you again, darling? Do you want to feel the fire?"

She rocked her ass from side to side in unspoken demand for what he offered. But he wasn't willing to accept her silence. He wouldn't be as magnanimous as he once had been. He'd allowed her secrets, allowed her not to speak about things that bothered her when she didn't want to. Perhaps the real mistake had been he'd never pressed her, never demanded more than she was willing to give freely. Maybe she needed a little push. Mayhap she needed to have him take all the control.

He scored the rosy ass cheek with his nails, not hard enough to leave a mark, but enough to know he sent tingling sensations up her body. "You have to say it, Chandra. Unlike before, when you were my lover and we had an understanding of sorts, tonight you have to tell me what you want."

"Don't do this, Simon, please." But she rocked her ass again.

"Don't what? Would you like me to stop? Or—"

"No." The reply burst from her. "Don't stop. Never stop."

"Then tell me, my love, what you want."

"Spank my bottom."

He chuckled and landed a second smack to the same cheek before moving to the other. "Always the proper lady. No one could imagine the vixen beneath the ladylike facade."

He alternated between slaps and caresses until her ass glowed red. While kissing her bare shoulder, he released her arms and gathered the dress over hips—careful not the let the fabric touch her sensitive ass—until it pooled on the floor. She clutched the bedding over her head.

"What do you want now? Tell me and I will give you anything."

In a small voice nearly too quiet to hear, she said, "Make love to me, here, like this."

Needing no other encouragement, he entered her in a swift movement that nearly caused him to come. He paused, not because it would make her crazy with lust, a plus for certain, but he didn't want to spill his seed before he was ready. The heat coming off her buttocks warmed his hips and groin, making it impossible to think or control his building desires.

She lifted on her elbows, changing the angle of their joined bodies. He drove into her over and over and she met him thrust for thrust, forcing him into her, deeper and harder. Finding her clit, he worked it while his cock filled her, sending her over the edge.

She screamed his name and fell into oblivion.

None too soon, Simon withdrew, spilling his seed in the palm of his hand. He'd debated coming inside her tonight. In that final minute, some deep-rooted caveman mentality demanded he impregnate her. She'd have no choice but to stay with him under those circumstances. But honor ruled it out. He might like to dominate their sex, with her permission, but he would never trap her, any more than she would trap him.

In the nearby basin, he washed, splashing the cool water over his flushed face before bringing a damp cloth to Chandra. She had yet to move, still breathing heavily from the orgasm, and shivered a bit as he pressed the cloth upon the heat of her ass.

"Are you all right?" he asked. He accepted her wordless nod. Once he'd helped her into the bed, he climbed in next to her, bringing her body into his to hold her. The same way he always had after they'd made love.

And for a minute, for that moment in time, he allowed himself to forget she had broken his heart.

Chapter Three

Tiny fireworks had gone off in her body and Chandra wondered if her world would ever be the same. Every stroke and thrust of Simon's had been meant to brand her, as he'd promised. To remind her she needed him, wanted him, and ached for him. Ultimately, the night felt like punishment of the best kind. Yet, as he held her firm to his chest, with his steady heartbeat in her ear like a soothing cadence, she didn't know if she had the strength to turn him away a second time.

"Should I apologize for being too rough?"

She shook her head. "No, I wanted it rough."

He shifted a bit. "If it hadn't been me here tonight, would you have allowed your 'date' to do that?"

He wanted her words. He always wanted her words. He'd told her once that many men were too stupid to listen to what women had to say, for they saw things of the world differently. Not better or worse, but from a different angle. And he'd learned a lot from seeing the other angles.

"Not like that, if at all. I thought I could, but in all honesty, I don't think so now. So many times today I thought of canceling. While waiting for your arrival this evening, I almost bolted an equal number of times."

His head rested on the headboard, his eyes closed, as if sleeping. But she knew well how he appeared when asleep and that wasn't it. He was contemplating, strategizing. She must take his mind off her and his desire to have her back. "And you would you have made love to whomever had been here?"

Not opening an eye, he said clearly, "I certainly would have tried."

She held her breath to keep from crying out at the emotional pain the five words caused. Of course he would have bedded whoever his mystery woman had been. He'd once told Chandra not to ask questions she wasn't prepared to hear the answer to. He'd also promised never to lie to her. And unless there was a very good reason for doing so, he would never keep a secret from her either.

Swallowing hard, she replied, "I shouldn't have asked."

"I didn't say I would have succeeded."

When she looked up at him, his deep brown eyes stared back.

"I don't understand," she said.

"That feeling I assume you just had, the one that took the glow from your eyes, as if hundreds of pounds of pressure are on your chest and someone was turning a knife in your gut; that was how I felt when I walked in tonight, knowing you were waiting for some stranger." Anger radiated from him and when he moved away from her to climb out of bed, she pulled the blanket up to her chin.

How could so much pain and anger be balled up in one man? He rarely displayed this side to her. And had never directed it at her, not even the night she'd rejected his hand. Closing eyelids heavy from weeks of strain and heartache, she allowed her mind to drift back to that evening as the memories flooded her.

They had lain on the floor before the fire, naked, listening to rain hit the windows, and enjoyed the empty house. Simon had rested his head in her lap, his hand brushing up and down the side of her exposed breast.

"You are insatiable."

"You wouldn't have me any other way."

"I will take you any way I can get you." She smiled down at him, running her fingers through his thick hair. "When can we meet again?"

His sigh told her no time soon. "I have to make a trip up to the family's northern estate. There are some issues which require my personal attention."

"Nothing serious, I hope."

"Serious enough for my estate manager to ask for my presence. Not ideal while the House of Lords is in season with laws on the floor that will affect my tenants and everyone on the border of Scotland. I can only hope Andrew and Wolfe can hold off the vote until I return."

"What can I do to help?"

"Come with me?"

"Be serious."

"I am serious. Come with me."

"As what? Your secretary? Your mistress?"

"My wife."

Ice filled her veins. Dread ate at her soul. "That's not funny, Simon."

Rolling up on to an elbow to better see her, he cupped her cheek. "I'm in earnest, Chandra. Marry me. Come with me and we can make a quick detour into Gretna Green and get married over the anvil."

"I can't."

"So maybe the anvil was too much." He gave her the same smile he had used to get her out into the garden on their first night. "If you prefer, I'll have the banns read, and we can wed when we return."

"Simon, I can't marry you."

"Would it help if I declared my love for you?"

No, it wouldn't help, her soul screamed even as her heart broke. If things had been different, if *she* were different, his offer would be everything she could hope for. A second chance at love. But life was a cruel maiden, and she didn't allow one to be so happy. Shaking her head, Chandra tried to turn away. Simon wouldn't let her.

"We've never spoken of feelings before, but I thought it was perfectly clear how I felt for you. Am I wrong? Do you care nothing for me.?"

"It isn't that easy. Of course I care for you." More than care; she loved him with every fiber of her being. But she wouldn't marry him. Couldn't bear it if his adoration died in their marriage bed. Then she would be trapped with a man who had every reason to hate her. "Marriage isn't something I have thought much on since my husband died. To be honest, I thought I would live the rest of my life as a merry widow."

He sat upright to stare at her. "Are you rejecting my suit?"

She nodded, unable to say the words, but by not speaking, she'd denied herself the one thing she wanted more than anything else. He shot to his feet and paced, before halting. And for the first time since she'd know him, he seemed unable to form a complete sentence.

"Simon, let's keep on the way we are. I am happy. But if you prefer, I could officially become your mistress." One little lie wouldn't kill her. Would it?

"Please explain to me, Mrs. Mallory, why you would prefer fucking me in private to marrying me in public. Is the only thing you want from me my cock?"

She frowned. "That was crude."

"And asking to become my mistress over wife wasn't?" Piece by piece, he gathered his discarded clothing. "Forgive me for being unable to see past that."

"Are you saying you wanted all of your past mistresses for more than their bodies?"

"You. Are. Different." He ground out each word between clenched teeth. "And you damned well know that. We have a mutually beneficial relationship. I do not pay your living expenses, and you do not sleep with me for the depth of my pockets."

"I seriously doubt your mistresses' only reason for sleeping with you was your money."

"I can't believe we are talking about this at all." He sliced the air with a hand, as if done with the whole conversation, and headed toward the door.

"Simon, why do we have to ruin something so wonderful?"

He paused, but didn't look at her, his body radiating barely contained fury. "My apologies for ruining it with a marriage proposal."

"You know I care about you."

"I love you, Chandra. Do you understand that? I. Love. You. I want you with me every night, not only those when I can sneak in like a thief in the night."

I love you, too! Her soul screamed loud enough she feared he could hear it. "How am I supposed to respond to that?"

"Forget I asked." His sudden calm sent shivers down her spine. "I won't make the same mistake again. Will you be staying, or shall I dampen the fire?"

So cool, so cold. Yet the roaring fire did little to warm her. "As soon as I am dressed, I will leave."

"Do you require my assistance?"

40

She shook her head, uncaring if she did. His demeanor was so frigid, she couldn't bear the thought of him touching her again.

"Very well. Should you need anything, you know how to get in touch with me. Shall I call when I return?"

"No, I think—that is…."

"You wish to end it?"

No, I wish to grow old in your arms. "I think it's for the best."

"A minute ago, you were offering to become my mistress. Now you wish to end things?

She nodded, unable to meet his eyes or speak. How could he understand what she didn't herself? But if they stayed together, with whatever title they chose to put on it, he would grow to hate her as George had. Oh, her late husband had never come out and said as much, but he'd stopped coming to her at night, and hadn't joined her for many months before his death. At meals, he'd seemed distant, not speaking or making eye contact. She couldn't bear the thought of Simon ever treating her in the same manner.

41

"I see." He strode to the window, never once turning from whatever he stared out at. She had broken him. It didn't matter if she had done it for all the right reasons. She had hurt the man she loved and she'd never stop regretting it.

Worse, he'd never seen it coming. The shock when she'd denied him couldn't have been faked. His proposal might not have been as romantic as her first, but it'd had more heart. The idea had obviously never crossed his mind she might refuse his suit. Being his bed partner for as long as she had been, sharing what they had both physically and emotionally, it was to be expected under the circumstances that they might wed. As a widow, she had more freedom than most other woman, but he hadn't been wrong to think she would accept. What *wasn't* there to want about him?

After dressing, she left before he did. He didn't acknowledge her departure. She walked home in the rain, unsure which drops sliding down her face were rain and which were tears. She only knew she was drowning.

Two weeks passed before word circulated that

Simon had returned to town, amid rumors he was tearing anyone and anything in his path into pieces. She went to the townhouse and waited for him, even though she had ended their affair. Returning every day for a week, she hoped he would come and prayed he would stay away. As she prepared to leave her house one morning, a messenger in Simon's black and green livery arrived with a gift for the lady of the house. .

Thanking the man, she took the package into her sitting room, her hands trembling as she opened the ornate box. A perfect set of diamond earrings and matching necklace lay in a bed of black velvet. She dreaded reading the card, knowing the jewels were meant as insult over affection. In the time they had been together, Simon had mentioned, on more than one occasion, how nice it was to be with a woman who didn't expect or even want expensive jewels as a thank you for services rendered. Being with her was the first time he had been with any woman who simply wanted to be with him and not his money or title.

Chandra, I knew when I saw these they would complement the ivory tone of your naked skin. As tempted as I am by your offer to be my mistress, I respectfully decline. May your next protector, as I assume you are now in the market for one, harden his heart better against your graces than I.

S.

Unable to stomach having the gems in her house, she called for a hackney and returned the *gift* to the store where Simon had purchased it. Upon orders from *the gentlemen* who paid for them, the proprietor had not allowed her to leave without taking the money the gems were worth. Surprised to find Simon knew she would return the set crushed her, but that he forced her to keep the money for it if she did was an insult beyond measure. As if she had spent two years as his whore. While contemplating how to throw his money in his face, she left the store and overheard two women speaking in hushed voices. One of them spoke about an evening she'd spent, set up by a Madame Eve.

Begging the women's pardon for eavesdropping,

Chandra left a while later with a calling card and a plan. What better way to spend Simon's money than on a date with another man? But, as soon as she sent her letter of inquiry to the matchmaker, she knew nothing ever went as planned.

Coming out of her musings of their shared past, Chandra was surprised to find Simon staring at her, concern edging his noble brow.

"You were deep in thought. What worries you?"

"What doesn't worry me, these days?" She attempted a smile, but it felt the way she did—terrible.

"What bothers you, love?"

Don't be kind to me, not now. "I fear if we are together even for this one night, you will never relent. We can't return to the way it was. You must marry and I know being here when you do will tear me apart."

"I will never marry unless you are the one standing with me before the minister." The vehemence in his voice brooked no argument.

"You must marry."

"Not unless you are my bride."

"You are the most thickheaded—" Without finishing the sentence, she grabbed the pillow behind her and hurled it at him in frustration. He simply stood, hands on his naked hips, and allowed the feathered sack to hit his chest and fall to the floor. Grabbing another, she threw it, too, repeating the action until nothing remained to lob at him..

"Are you done, or would you like me to gather your ammunition, should you care to have another go at it?"

"Stop trying to placate me!"

"Who's placating? I completely understand the need to take out some frustration. If you recall, I tore the damned sleeve almost clean off my tailcoat when I first arrived. My valet is going to have a fit. Yet, under the same circumstances, I would do it all over again." He scooped up the pillows and tossed them on the bed. "Your weapons, my love."

He stood before her in all his glory, and she wondered what to do with him. Moving the cushions out of the way, she found the neckcloth he had removed earlier. Wrapping the silky tie around her hands, she knew exactly what she wanted to do.

"Come here," she commanded.

His eyebrow rose at her assertive tone. Taking the two steps separating them, he gazed down at her. "I am here."

"Do you trust me?"

"With my heart."

God, he always had known the right thing to say. "Lie down."

"Very well." He climbed into the bed and sprawled against the bolster. Lifting a leg over his hips, she straddled him and kissed him hard. He had always been the one in control while she'd taken on the more submissive roll during their previous lovemaking. But, tonight, she wanted to take the lead. "Put your arms above your head."

After a slight hesitation, he obeyed. "If I allow you to do this," he said, starting to give her one hand, "I want something from you."

"If it is in my power, I will give you anything"

"At the end of our lovemaking, you will tell me why you refused my suit."

"But...."

"No buts. I have waited long enough."

"Very well. But if you at any time attempt to take control, I will leave this room immediately, and you will agree never to see me again."

"Are you insane? I can't make that promise to you. Not after tonight."

She shrugged. "Mayhap that was a bit extreme."

"Mayhap?"

"All right. If you take control without my permission, you will never again ask me to marry you."

"If I let you have your way, you understand I will continue to ask. I will never let up."

She nodded. Then, doing the one thing she'd never truly expected him to agree to, he placed both hands above his head and closed his eyes. "Do your worst."

As she moved up his body to secure his wrists to the thick wood post of the bed, her breast came within

48

reach of his mouth. Never being one to miss the opportunity to suck her bosom, he took a nipple into his mouth. *Oh, how divine.* It took her a few seconds to come to her senses and remember she was in charge.

"You haven't earned the right to touch me quite yet," she said.

He arched one regal brow. "Earned?"

Earned did seem a bit strong, seeing as she would gladly give him any part of her. She yearned for it, except then she couldn't think, and she wanted him so filled with desire he could go mad with it. With no real idea how to proceed, she needed to have him at her mercy. Even for a few moments in time.

"Are you comfortable?"

He tugged on the restraint. "You must be joking."

Smiling, she understood why he balked. For Simon, a man in charge of all aspects of his life, to give her such power was contrary to every fiber of his being. Yet, he submitted to her will. Should he want to get free, he had the ability to do so in a matter of seconds. She couldn't tie a knot to save her life, but it didn't matter. He'd given her what she wanted—control. Perhaps, when she finished with him, he would acquiesce and allow her to become his mistress. She could never be his wife, but she would have him for her lover for as long as he allowed.

After sitting back to admire her less-than-handy work, she brushed her lips over his and ground against his hard cock. He jerked his arms and gripped the silk fabric binding his hands. If he continued, she feared he might rip it. Running a calming hand down his chest, she savored every touch of the sculptured arms and chest, so perfect, as if he'd been chiseled out of marble from the heavens above. Every muscle jumped in response when she scraped her nails lightly up the underside of his arms, then over his shoulders and sides.

"Are you trying to punish me?" His voice sounded deeper and harsher than normal.

"What did you tell me once? Oh, let me think…." She relished his groan as he arched his back. "I believe your exact words were…." Bending forward, she whispered into his ear, 'There can be unbelievable pleasure in punishment.'" She nipped his earlobe and increased the pressure of her nails on his abdomen.

Taking her time, she kissed and tasted her way down the bare skin laid before her like a feast. As his groans deepened and his breathing hastened, she grew bolder. Moving until her mouth was level with his fully aroused cock, she glanced up at his face and met his eyes, so full of heat and lust. She wrapped a hand around his erection and, without breaking eye contact, took the tip into her mouth.

He threw his head back and cursed, words that should have caused her to blush. But, at that moment, the same words drove her. Opening her lips wider, she worked down his shaft. When her eyes watered, she eased up until only the head of his cock touched her lips. She laved him, tasting the salty juices. Simon yanked at the bindings around his wrists and the bedpost creaked. Spurred on by his inner struggle and inability to escape, she took her time, reveling in the pleasure she gave him. He bucked his hips, but she doubted he had any awareness of the action or could have controlled it if he did. Finally, she repositioned herself until no part of her touched his body.

His ragged breathing slowed and he opened his eyes. With a moan, he said, "Christ. You can't leave me like this."

"What is it you want?"

He yanked on the restraint again. "You."

"I need your words, Simon. I need you to tell me what you want me to do."

Glaring at her, he ground out, "I want that beautiful mouth on my cock again. I want you to take me so deep you can't breathe."

Those are certainly some words.

"Damn it, Chandra! Please."

She didn't wait for him to beg again. When her lips replaced her hand around him, he rewarded her with another moan that vibrated through him. She tasted his arousal as more of his seed leaked from his cock. Licking her way from base to tip, she took him deep into her throat one last time and massaged his balls while she used her tongue to drive him to near bedlam. When his body tightened, she drew back.

"Fuck." He strained to lift his head off the pillow for a better view of her. "Chandra, allow me my release. Allow me to touch you."

She shook her head and returned her focus to his body.

"God, yes—like that. Ah, hell." The bed rattled under them as he jerked the ties. "Damn it, please, Chandra—finish this."

Breaking away, she smiled and licked her lips. "Shhh. Patience."

Straddling him again, she reached between them and positioned him at her wet opening. She took him deep inside her and caught her breath, loving how he stretched her, as always. Simon curved his hips upward, urging his cock deeper. She placed her hands on the wall above the bed and this time, when he rose to take her nipple into his mouth she didn't argue. She rode him, building the friction between them until her orgasm took over, powerful and earthshaking.

"Let me touch you," he begged.

She couldn't speak, only nodded into his

shoulder that she'd collapsed against seconds earlier. Before she could catch her breath, he jerked free of the ties and flipped her onto her back. The feral look in his eyes told her that she had pushed him to the very edge of his patience. He grasped her thigh, lifting her leg over his hip to open her wider to him. He'd told her he loved her in the same breath that promised to make her understand what she had done to him.

Chandra fell again, off the edge into ecstasy so intense, spots danced behind her eyes and she thought she might have blacked out briefly. At the last moment, like he always did, Simon pulled out, but rather than his seed landing in his hand, in a handkerchief, or on the bed, he released on her belly. How she wished he had remained inside her.

Chapter Four

Not being able to touch her had been excruciating. Simon needed control and always had. He'd been raised to run his lands, his seat in the House of Lords, and up until meeting Chandra, he'd felt in control of every aspect of his life. But she surprised him at every turn. What happened between them had gone in opposition of everything he held dear, yet for her he would go through it over and over again. Whatever it took to keep her with him, even if it fought against his very nature, he would make that sacrifice.

Rolling over, he threw his legs over the edge of the bed. He worked on steadying his breathing and wondered if the shaking was the world quaking in the aftermath of what had passed between them. How he'd imagined he could ever get over her, he didn't know.

"I am going to check on getting us a bath."

She didn't answer, but then he hadn't expected

her to. Walking into the adjoining room, he found a steaming bath waiting for him. He returned to the other room and carried her into the bathing chamber, lowered her into the water then followed her. In the past, he would have climbed in behind her, but this time he wanted to see her face. The tub had been built for two people and, after settling on the other side, facing her, he allowed her to prepare for what she needed to tell him. But she didn't speak.

When he could wait no longer, he whispered, "Chandra."

Not making eye contact, she stretched between them to rub his knees. "I know I promised you an explanation."

"Sometimes saying it fast makes it easier." He wondered what could be so difficult to tell him. Was she secretly married to someone else? The thought angered him. Unlike the last time they'd been together, she might not have vocalized her feelings, but he'd felt it in everything she did.

She nodded as if agreeing with his advice. "I can't marry you."

"So you have declared," he replied without hostility. Then waited to hear her out.

"I need you to understand."

"I am trying to." Taking her hands, he lowered his head so he could meet her eyes. "You can do this. Nothing you say to me will alter how I feel about you."

She focused on something behind him, perhaps the chair against the back wall, anything to prevent looking at him as if his words were too hard to take. Tears filled her eyes and she stiffened, appearing to brace herself to tell him the worst. "Simon, I'm barren."

He blinked. "And?"

"That's all you can say?"

He didn't know enough about the workings of the female body and childbearing to say much more. "I'm not sure what else to say. I mean, how can you be so sure?"

"I was married for a decade and never had a child. That in itself makes me sure." She tried to climb out of the tub, but he stilled her by placing a hand on her stomach; the heart of their problems.

He took her lips with his, not with passion, but love and understanding. "I only ask because I don't have all the information."

"I cannot condemn you to a life without an heir. I kept hoping I would get with child, but every month I discovered it was not to be."

"So, if you were pregnant…."

"I would pack tonight and head to Gretna Green without question. But unless I can give you an heir, I will not risk marrying you."

He pondered her words. "Allow me to understand; you won't marry me until you are with child. We seem to have a problem then because I will not impregnate you until we are married. Our children will be created in our marriage bed."

"During my marriage, I lived through the humiliation, month after month, when my menses came. George never said anything, but I knew he felt disappointment in me for my failure. And then having to prove I wasn't increasing after George died added to my suffering. I couldn't stand watching the pity in the eyes of everyone and hearing the gossip that his wife was barren."

"Has it never occurred to you the issue might have been with George? That his disappointment was with himself, not you? From what you have told me about him, I would guess he was upset seeing you worry that you had failed him."

"Yes, but you and I have been intimate for close to two years and nothing."

Throwing his hands up, Simon returned to his side of the tub. "Because I have never spent my seed in you."

"I have heard talk that other women have gotten pregnant that way."

"Most never do. But I am wanting to marry *you*, not your womb." Placing his hands on her cheeks, he forced her to meet his eyes. He had to make her understand how much he loved and needed her. The last month without her had been the worst of his life.

"Chandra, what matters to me is us. Children would be wonderful, but I would rather have my brother inherit my title and lands now if it meant I could be with you. I promise I won't leave you unprotected like your first husband did."

"Simon—"

"Let me finish. I know you loved George, but I know you care for me as well. Perhaps you will never be able to love me like you did him. I can live with that. But I can't live without you." Standing, he offered a hand to help her to her feet and out of the tub. "I am insufferable to live with when you aren't around. I'm surprised I have any friends left, and, believe me, no one in Parliament wants to deal with me right now." He picked up a towel from a nearby table and bent to dry her legs.

"I heard rumors to that." She smiled down at him.

"It has not been pleasant." He peered up at her. "So?"

"Can I have a few days to think about it?"

He straightened, wanting to know what more she possibly have to think about, but bit back the question. Instead, he asked, "How much time do you need?"

With surprise in her clear eyes, she asked, "A few days?"

"Did you get an invitation to Foxhaven's masquerade ball?" Simon walked backward out of the bathroom while leading her toward the bed because he didn't want to take his eyes off her .

"Yes, as did all of London."

Cupping her face, he said, "I want your answer then."

"Very well. I will send a message telling you what my costume will be so you can find me."

She seemed under the impression he couldn't find her in a costume, but he'd be able to find her with his eyes closed.

He lifted her into the bed. They had a few hours before the sun rose, and he would show her one last time why accepting his suit would be the best decision she had ever made. He needed her to realize he could love her enough for both of them.

Chapter Five

Where the hell was she?

Andrew and Wolfe had twice come to his side, trying to ascertain why he stalked the front entry hall. Simon had run out of excuses three friendly visits ago and his patience wouldn't hold out much longer. He'd arrived first. Luckily, Wolfe had been preoccupied and hadn't seemed to notice Simon, who never arrived to any ball on time, had shown up an hour early. Thus, the usually inquisitive duke hadn't said anything to him until they stood side by side, hours later, staring over the main hall.

"Who are you waiting for?" Wolfe scanned the room below them.

"Cleopatra. You?"

"I will know her when I see her."

For the first time that night, Simon truly looked at his close friend. The duke was actively hunting someone as well, and Simon suspected it might have something to do with Madame Eve. Perhaps he wore the same seeking expression Wolfe had. Or, maybe, because ever since his "date," Wolfe acted somehow different, less restless, yet more intent. But unless Simon admitted to procuring the woman's services for himself, he couldn't ask how Wolfe's own date had gone.

Simon smiled. "Best of luck to her."

"Yes, yours, too. Ah, is that Cleo herself?"

Simon snapped his head around and his breath caught, his body responding as it always did at the sight of his lover. "Yes, it is."

"Interesting." Wolfe clapped his shoulder before driving through the crush to be lost in the sea of the ton.

Chandra stood in the open hallway for a second, fidgeting with the drawstring bag around her wrist before moving toward one of the side rooms. Simon worked his way around the hall and out of sight in one of the alcoves and waited. Once she was within reach, he snaked an arm around her waist to pull her within the confines of the secluded, curtained area.

She gasped as his mouth descended and he kissed

her hard. Only a few days had passed, but he hadn't slept well, images of her flooding his mind, as had questions and concerns he might lose her.

"Simon," she whispered against his lips.

"Hello, love." He took a moment to play with a loose tendril of hair falling over her shoulder. "What's your answer?"

"You do not waste time, do you?"

His gaze flickered up to hers. "We've wasted enough."

"I need to tell you something before I give you my answer."

"Someone is likely to find us in here. Come with me." Holding her hand, he tugged her through the crowded ballroom out to the back gardens. "The maze."

Moving beyond the area lit with Chinese lanterns, they entered the dark recesses of the tall hedges that created walled walkways and turns. He took the maze's puzzle by memory. They didn't speak until they were safely in the center of it.

"I will never find my way out," she said.

After removing his mask, he did the same with hers. What needed to be said wouldn't happen behind the coverings. "I will always make sure you find your way."

"I need to tell you that I love you," she said in a rush. When he moved in to embrace her, she stilled him with a palm on his chest. "No, let me speak because I will never be able to say everything I need to if you kiss me again."

"Would you like to sit?" He indicated the stone bench in the center.

"No."

"Would you like me to sit?"

Her face was barely visible in the moonlight, but he caught the slight nod. She waited for him to settle on the bench before starting.

"I loved my first husband and I don't wish to speak ill of the dead, but I was quite young when I married him. I didn't understand many things. George was sweet and kind. He came to me when the need came over him and I would dutifully lie there until he was done. He would then go back into his

65

bedchamber."

Simon wanted to announce he wouldn't be accepting that kind of relationship but waited patiently for her to continue. "The only thing George wanted from me was an heir to carry on his name and acquire his lands. I failed him and I was very afraid I would fail you, too."

"You could never fail me by being my wife."

"I know that now, but it has taken me a long time to believe that."

Hope flared within him. "What are you trying to say?"

"I am saying I want to live my life again. I want to be in love. I need you, and if you are willing to take a chance on us, I can do no less."

It took two short steps to get to her. Bringing her into his arms, he promised to never let her go. "Will you marry me?"

"Yes."

"Tomorrow?"

"Yes. If you can arrange it."

"It's already arranged. I spoke to the archbishop

yesterday." Simon's face burned and he was thankful Chandra couldn't see it in the dim light.

"A bit high-handed, even for you, don't you think?" Her tone held some annoyance, but he didn't miss the hint of relief in her words.

"Perhaps, but I couldn't stand the thought you might change your mind. I had to be prepared." Holding her gloved hand, he undid the delicate pearl buttons on the inside of her wrist and exposed the pale skin beneath. Bringing it to his lips, he placed a soft kiss above her pulse. "When it comes to keeping you in my life, the lengths I am willing to go may surprise you."

"Thank you."

He paused. "Whatever for?"

"For loving me. For not taking no for an answer."

"I want you."

"You have me." She ran her fingers through his hair.

"No. I want you now. Here."

She glanced back at the only way out of the center of the maze. "Anyone could come across us."

"Not anyone. Very few people besides Wolfe and myself can make it through this maze in the dark. And Wolfe's interests lie with some mystery woman. When he finds her, I doubt he will be heading out here, not when he has the ducal bed upstairs waiting for them." Simon traced the neckline of Chandra's bodice. Lingered in the line of her cleavage.

Breathless, she lifted her face to him. "This is unwise."

"We will hear anyone else coming long before they get here." Simon didn't care if they were discovered. She was his betrothed and, by this time tomorrow, she would be his wife.

Chandra bit her lip and glanced over her shoulder again, exposing the elegant line of her neck. "I think we should—"

Such a temptation was too much for him to ignore. He didn't want to hear what they should or should not do. The only way to prevent her from speaking would be to take her breath away. He grasped her nape, pulled her into him, and kissed her. Unlike their last evening together, he was able to relax into the kiss. He didn't feel he must fight to keep their life together. He didn't have to prove anything, only show her he loved her.

Although society frowned on couples wearing their hearts on their sleeves, he didn't care. He planned to make it known to all that she was taken and he wanted the mamas he had softly brushed off over the last two years to see he had no interest in marrying their virginal daughters, nor having a tryst with the mamas themselves. The ring he would put on Chandra's hand would take care of their speculation.

"You're smiling," she observed.

"I'm happy. For more reasons than you can imagine. Shall we announce our impending wedding?"

"No. Let's surprise everyone." She threw her arms around him again and kissed him.

A giggle came from nearby, closer than Simon was ready for. In that moment, he wanted the announcement of their wedding to be honorable and not clouded in gossip. Breaking away from Chandra, he shoved her behind him. Not a second later, two intertwined bodies came into view, one of which he recognized.

"Andrew?" He enjoyed the same scene play out as his friend shoved his companion behind him and out of sight, though Simon suspected Andrew's reasoning had more to do with not being caught in the matrimonial noose than on protecting her honor.

"What the hell are you doing out here?" Andrew asked.

"Looking for some privacy," Simon drawled.

"So I see." Andrew called out, "Good Evening, Mrs. Mallory."

Chandra shifted from behind Simon. "Lord Windenshire."

Simon glanced back and forth between Chandra and his friend. "You two know each other?"

She laughed. "You didn't think you were the only lord I knew, did you?"

Andrew hid his own laugh behind his hand and an obvious cough. Simon glared at him before facing Chandra, who gave him a cheeky grin. "No, I didn't think that. It does surprise me to know you are well-acquainted with this rakehell."

"No need for name slinging." Andrew said, then drew his companion into the maze. "If it's all the same to you both, we will seek another, quite private retreat."

"By your leave," Simon replied.

Andrew nodded at Chandra. "Mrs. Mallory, a pleasure as always."

"Milord. Perhaps you would like to come by Simon's London home tomorrow." She looked at Simon for a confirmation of the time.

He smiled, bringing her hand to his lips. "About two."

"I wouldn't miss it for the world." With that, Andrew gave a slight bow and whisked his lady friend back the way they had come.

"You'll excuse me if I'm thrilled that will be the last time I hear you referred to as 'Mrs. Mallory.'"

"I have carried that name for so long and still I find I am anxious to try out my new name and title. I fear it will take me a bit to get used to."

Cupping her face, he said, "I will be there every

step of the way to help you feel comfortable in your new life. I will stand by you, support you, and guide you. All you have to do is ask."

"Tomorrow cannot come fast enough. I fear something will burst this bubble of happiness I feel."

"As do I. But I am willing to make sure it doesn't." He led her out of the hedge maze, the years of doing it blindfolded helping him maneuver though the turns. Rather than heading toward the ballroom, he took the path around the large house to the side entrance that led to the main square. "Come home with me tonight. Stay in my arms until daylight breaks, never leave my side until we say 'I will' in front of the minister."

She nodded her confirmation and placed her head on his shoulder.

Hand in hand and without speaking, they walked the block required to get to his family home. At the foot of the stairs he kissed her again, only stopping when he heard the slight clearing of a throat from the landing above. His butler, Wallace, greeted them with a smile, and to his new mistress, he bowed, welcoming her to her new home.

"We can tour the house tomorrow. Wallace, we are not to be disturbed." Bending down, Simon lifted Chandra into his arms and said to the butler, "First thing in the morning, please send some servants to pack up your mistress's house. I believe you know the address. And the minister is due here by two, so please inform Cook to have a spread ready."

"Yes, milord."

Simon took the steps two at a time, striding down hallways he knew she would never remember. Finally arriving at his bedchamber, he found candles lit for his return. Lowering her to her feet, he nuzzled her ear. "Tomorrow, you become my marchioness, but tonight I will make you my wife."

Chandra said nothing, but he suspected she understood his meaning. In this room, her actions spoke louder than words. With each kiss, every touch, she let him know she loved him.

In the morning, he would have to send a thank-you note to Madame Eve for bringing Chandra back into his life. And, perhaps, when their first daughter made her appearance they would name her Evangeline. For now, however, he focused on loving and cherishing this woman and thanking the good Lord above that he'd been given a second chance to win her over.

Reaching a palm out to her, Simon said, "Come, my love, to our bed. Let us start as we mean to continue. Side by side."

"Together." She placed her hand in his and followed his lead. "I love you, Simon, and I always will."

Masculine pride flowed through him and her words nearly brought him to his knees with their potency. He undressed them both, helping her into the bed before he followed. Kissing her bare shoulder, he pulled her back into his embrace. Her soft backside fit perfectly against his front. Although his cock hardened and demanded to be taken care of, Simon was content to hold her. He had years to prove her wrong about her inability to create a child. In that moment, nothing else mattered, not his lust or fears about procreating. It was about them; one woman and one man, in love.

Beyond that, nothing mattered.

About the Author

Award-winning author Dominique Eastwick grew up a US Navy Brat, so if there was a naval base, that was probably home. She currently resides in North Carolina with her husband, two children, crazy lab and lazy cat.

Dominique's love of reading started when she was told to read *To Kill a Mockingbird* in high school—a book that opened her eyes to the joys of reading and entering into the world of the author. To this day she ranks this book as her favorite.

Also by Dominique Eastwick

Strawberry Kisses

The Duke and the Virgin

The Earl and His Virgin Countess

Shifting Hearts

Healing His Soul's Mate

Infiltrating Her Pack

www.ingramcontent.com/pod-product-compliance
Lightning Source LLC
Chambersburg PA
CBHW072040170626
46811CB00008B/3116